AF214550

Don't let down

your guard

until he's shown

you he has the makings of a king

-guard

There's many funerals
you have to attend
because you killed
people with your kindness
when they expected you to fight

-the better person

Anger is

the silent killer

people disguise

in tears

Her happiness
shouldn't be possible

In a world so
cruel
with intentions

but here she is walking
through the storm

here she is

smiling as if hell doesn't exist.

-positive person

It is love that

carries rain

either to grow

a garden

or wash it all away

- be careful who you let be your raincloud

Give me a wildflower
and i will wonder how anyone
could pluck the making
of magic?

-will you destroy me too

I assumed being human

was about hiding the humanness in me

as if the sweat, tears and blood

would ruin me

when actually being human

is admitting they are

a sign of being alive

-just alive

Of all the lights i've ever witnessed

you are the only kind

who is bright enough

to lead me out of the dark

and dim enough

as to not burn my eyes

-light in the dark

Calm shores remind me

of evenings indoors in which

the cat is asleep,

the dog is lazy

and my heart is excited

for the morning.

-shore

Beauty
Only matters
When you
Know it.

-you know you're beautiful

I'm certain you could

climb a whole mountain top,

swim to the bottom of an abyss and back

and they'd still just shrug

with blankness in their eyes

as if you only got back

from the grocery store

-support yourself

Some spend too long fighting
a war with themselves
that even kindness
seems like shellshock.

-shellshock

Casual

I hope death

is casual

as if going to the store

to buy carrots

but coming back with ice-cream

or thinking you'll flunk

an essay paper

but receiving an A.

She's made of
electricity

having the perfect ability
to spark a fire

or save a life.

-fire

I find myself

rooting for change

on social media,

but without a protest

without our voices shouting

into the sky

we have failed

and are simply

leading each other

to slaughter.

-        Protest

Do not give her the burden
of saving the world
when she is in the madness
of saving herself

- therapy

"He's an overthinker"

they said

as if that beautiful mind

is broken

for carrying what if's and maybe's

-Overthinker

I adore flowers for opening
 their lips to the break of dawn
like singers in a choir
praising with hymns of salvation
saved for summer days
before the fall winds brush their happiness away
I too rise in the morning
unfurling my petals
to the sunlight
unaware that times will come to break me,
that death too will leave a mark
but still what is the point
of living life thinking about the coming sadness
when i could live a life
filled with
blissful joy

-flowers in summer

I pray you occasionally give

space for doubts,

 sometimes

trying the jump will only leave more

room for pain

-not achieving everything is okay

I said i forgive you
so how can i still remember
the pain

it took years to figure out
that both are separate

just like a flower remembers
a temporary drought

-forgive

"Do you forgive me?"

Of course i

forgive you

like a flower forgives the drought

who stole its strength

like a town forgives the tsunami

who crashed its life

of course i forgive you

i always will

but that doesn't mean i'll forget

the fire that burned me.

Some gifts are best left anticipated

than received

because the wait is like christmas eve

You don't have to capture her heart

to win her over,

      just give her a vacation

in the form of your presence

-vacation

The stars remind me
that from afar
someone may look
like all we desire
and want
but up close may be the very fire
that leaves you burned

-starlight

I gaze at the storm outside
wishing, like lightning,
that my heart can
make noise that's heard

-thunder

when the anger settles
I want to rip it out, carry it to safety
away from their judgments

who are they to judge my anger
when they were the ones who
placed it in my chest
while i begged them
"no"

-angry

You deserve someone who takes a step back

not out of disgust

but admiration

-stunning

A gentle tide submerged
barefeet
 on sandy shores,
and for one split second
she felt the sensation
of not just living
but being alive.

-shore

Just because

he lied

does not mean you

were dumb for believing him

you only wanted to believe the good

Give your heart time
to grow back in place
because even if it's slightly crooked
it'll still love the same.

Some fires in the heart
can't be lit
by him
and it's okay
perfectly okay
 to sit by
the warmth you built yourself

-warmth

If you expect her to change

for you

you have just as much luck

expecting a villain

to surrender

-        Villain

The love i carry
becomes heavy

yet still with every muscle
I fight to keep it

steady

Dear sadness,
my relationship with you
will always be complicated
like an ex stopping by for a visit unannounced
in which i am given two choices:

let you back
one
more time

or tell you to
"back off"

but my mind always wants to give second
chances for what has caused me pain
because my heart wants to always see
the light in a devil's eyes

-inviting sadness

People carry energies
so it only makes sense
that you disconnect
for a little while

-anti-social

Scientists say

ghosts don't exist

but why the hell

do i still feel your

hatred

years later

-ghosts

They will never stop
hating

even if you smile,
especially when you smile

but you never have to absorb
their energy

- positive vibes only

Success isn't about making it big
it's about making
your demons look small
in comparison

-fighting the fire

He's convinced that love is
sacrifice

but she never wanted
him to trade his world
to live in hers

-giving the world away

My heart isn't made of gold

instead it

resembles a 1920's newspaper

reporting on wild souls

who dance

the charleston

in the rain

-my heart is wild

I don't need your pity

    I get enough of that from myself

-sadness hits me occasionally

She isn't mean
for telling you her boundaries

you are the manipulator
for assuming
she doesn't have any

-manipulator

I will not change my persona

for a man

who cannot

handle the liveliness of an ocean

resting in my soul

-he can't handle the deep

I feel your anger
like knives

and i can do nothing
but fight the fire

with fire

-What else can I do?

Only people

counting on your downfall

see you

as competition

-i'm not competition

You could give her the whole
world
wrapped with apologies
and she'd still know her worth enough
to say "i forgive you but no"

-he gets no second chances

How dare they

act like my body

can lose it's worth

based off of how many men

have attempted to steal

my roots but only left

with a leaf

to remind them of their failures

- we are not defined by manipulation

Just because you see good in the monster

does not mean he's worth risking

a chance for

when he thought it was ok

to be a monster at all

-beauty and the beast

The marigolds aren't quite as pretty

as i once thought,

shifting in the earth

a reminder of my mind

that i too will die

like them

i too will be plucked from my roots

put in a glass

just to be deemed *undesirable*

and thrown away

once my liveliness fades.

-marigolds

I wish i could talk about that

time of my life

without people asking "well are you better now"

as if i can just step over a line

and watch the past fade

like falling leaves

because the pain might always

be a memory,

       a part of my story

       but it was sure as hell never who i was.

-past

Fear drives
me out of crowded rooms.

People are like stories
with unknown endings

and i've always hated
reading a book i can't finish.

-socializing.

It's hard to get close
to others
when they expect you
to uncover your heart
but never prepare themselves
to see the pain.

-pain

I admire the types of love

where no words

are spoken

yet

not even constellations could

hold what is felt.

-felt

Pale

You are pale in comparison
to the depth i found in words
for
never could i swim in the
lyrics of your mind.

Yes

She craves the stillness

associated with love

the kind of love

that expects nothing

but an answer back.

Foreign

Her body
feels foreign after
that.
when i say
that
I mean the distrust you weaved
into her spine,
the lies you folded into her heart
like pastry dough
and the many flames you made
just to
say there was a spark
when in reality
you started a forest fire
in her.

Butterflies

When i first started reading

poetry

I expected butterflies

in my heart to lead

my soul always back to you,

not that i would

be convinced so softly

to leave

 for me.

Sorry i haven't texted you back
the demons caught me
and stole my energy to live
or feel anything
at all
and i'm just now trying to feel
okay
i'm just now trying to feel something
anything
at all
even if that feeling
Is a conversation with you

-ghost

I want the words i write

to have a certain power

In them

that they will remind

people in this world that

they are what makes the world beautiful.

-world

Even flowers grow through
cracks in the pavement
but the question is how
do they grow
in a jail courtyard
where the sun shines above the
fenced walls taunting about
freedoms outside?

can't the weary soul's outside
of this confinement see that they are confined too
in a world so keen on death and
suffering
in a world so set on war.

yet flowers bloom in the darkest places
deepest caverns, and weirdest crevasses
but i do not know how they get there, growing in
rebellious glory
for all to see

I see their magic

I see their brilliance

I see their daily reminder that we are all confined

somewhat but it is up to us to water ourselves

and grow through any box that was given for us

to fit into.

-mental prison

I am afraid that i will become
what i fear,
that anger will slowly grow in
my heart
 and nestle until
I become strangely
 comfortable with it.

-fighting anger

Don't tell me

not to cry

when you caused my tears

like a snake you tell me

not to

remove the venom

you bit

 into me

You asked
 if i loved you,
  I muttered "I don't know"
you replied
  "Love is as simple as reading a book,
  You either feel it or you don't"
so i whispered back
   "You are the whole library
    disguised as a soul"

-library

I do not want

this if you

will always secretly

want another

       why desire the moth

when you already have a butterfly?

we

as women

so often weave our bodies

into what other people say we are

       a rug for others to walk over,

       a blanket to keep kings warm when it should
be ourselves,

       a net for men to use

when we are actually

tapestries filled with

hidden stories

and magic

meant to be there for ourselves

to go down in history

as the ones who healed the neighboring

lands with our visions

and healing

with our guiding hands

and healing balms.

Gold rims your heart

promising me of what could be

if i chose you

but what you didn't tell me was that

It was all fake.

-fools gold

We last

like taffy,

sweet and sugary

but no glue to keep us together

or nutrition to help us grow.

There is power

in the way you

showed them

no attention

when they

taunted your

powerful mind

like a game.

-power

no,

love does not hurt

in the process of growing.

it holds your pieces

together

while the world

whispers to "fall apart"

Many are afraid of her

fire

and that is how

it should be

She has a piano heart

with music desired by many

but only touched

by one.

Love doesn't beg to work out

It just sticks

like post it notes

on refrigerator

doors

reminding you

to drink water

and take your meds.

what a tragedy
to be part of
the dance
but never feel
the joys of dancing
to watch others smile
and wonder if
any of them feel deep down
like
dancing through life
is useless
during a heartstorm?

-part of the dance

silence

isn't an enemy

it is a friend

brought to you

when you have

no words to speak

sometimes the best word

is nothing.

-nothing

I held a butterfly in my hand
and she told me
"I was still beautiful
as a caterpillar
not because of
what i looked like
but because i knew who
 i was meant to be
before i grew wings &
flew.

-butterfly

I'm not "gifted"
with words
i'm responsible
with them

If i dared to love myself
the whole hill would be silenced

those tossing stones
would *stop*

for one second
and realize they

are tossing
stones

at a flowered wall.

-flowered

I am happy

sadness shrieked
and buried itself
to escape my light

The best love poems

written

don't rush like a wind

     destroying

         breaking

     killing with emotions

     that you have no words for

it is subtle

a stillness you find in

togetherness

that could fade at any time

     and that's what makes it so exciting

to be loved by him

to be apart of love

     and risk forever

 with now.

-best love poems

Sometimes there's strength
in moving that boulder
alone
just to prove
the monsters
you could.

The scariest things
aren't farthest from human,
but the things that we are afraid
we could become
In certain situations.

Some men will fight a
 whole damn war
creating a trojan horse
to battle for you to come back
instead of
reminding you of what home looks like
away from the storm.

If you want to fight for her, put down the armor

-armor